CW00802938

Before reading

Look at the book cove

Ask, "What do you thir

Turn to the **Key Words** on page

the child. Draw their attention to the shape of the letters, ... ng

the tall letters and those that have a tail.

During reading

Offer plenty of support and praise as the child reads the story. Listen carefully and respond to events in the text.

When a **Key Word** is used for the first time, it is also shown at the bottom of the page. If the child hesitates over a word, point to the **New Key Words** box and practise reading it together. If the word is phonically decodable, you can sound out the letters and blend the sounds to read the word ("d-o-g, dog"). Praise the child for their effort, then return to the story.

Pause every few pages and ask questions to check the child's understanding of what they have read. If they begin to lose concentration, stop reading and save the page for later.

Celebrate the child's achievement and come back to the story the next day.

After reading

After reading this book, ask, "Did you enjoy the story? What did you like about it?" Encourage the child to share their opinions.

Use the comprehension questions on page 54 to check the child's understanding and recall of the text.

Ladybird

Series Consultant: Professor David Waugh
With thanks to Kulwinder Maude

LADYBIRD BOOKS

UK | USA | Canada | Ireland | Australia
India | New Zealand | South Africa

Ladybird Books is part of the Penguin Random House group of companies
whose addresses can be found at global.penguinrandomhouse.com.
www.penguin.co.uk   www.puffin.co.uk   www.ladybird.co.uk

Original edition of Key Words with Peter and Jane first published by Ladybird Books Ltd 1964
Series updated 2023
This book first published 2023
002

Text copyright © Ladybird Books Ltd, 1964, 2023
Illustrations by Nuno Alexandre Vieira, Flora Aranyi, and Fran and David Brylewski
Based on characters and design by Gustavo Mazali
Illustrations copyright © Ladybird Books Ltd, 2023

Printed in China

The authorized representative in the EEA is Penguin Random House Ireland,
Morrison Chambers, 32 Nassau Street, Dublin D02 YH68

A CIP catalogue record for this book is available from the British Library

ISBN: 978-0-241-51079-7

All correspondence to:
Ladybird Books
Penguin Random House Children's
One Embassy Gardens, 8 Viaduct Gardens, London SW11 7BW

MIX
Paper from
responsible sources
FSC® C018179

Key Words

with Peter and Jane

3a

We like rabbits

Based on the original
Key Words with Peter and Jane
reading scheme and research by William Murray

Original edition written by William Murray
This edition written by Chitra Soundar
Illustrated by Nuno Alexandre Vieira, Flora Aranyi,
and Fran and David Brylewski
Based on characters and design by Gustavo Mazali

at   car   dad

for   get   go

he   home   into

mum   no   play

please   rabbit

that   this   to

we   with   yes

car

dad

home

mum

play

rabbit

Peter and Jane get into the car.

They are going to the shops.

New Key Words

get   into   car   go   to

"We can go into that shop to get jam for Peter," says Mum.

Peter wants to go into this shop.

He looks at the rabbits in this shop.

13

"Can we go into that shop, please?" says Jane.

"That shop? Yes," says Dad.

15

They go into the book shop.

"We can get a book on cars for Mum," Dad says.

Tess wants to go in.

"No, Tess. Come and get into the car, please!" says Mum.

no

"This book has rabbits in it. Please can we get this?" says Peter.

"Yes, we can get that. I can get this book on cars for Mum," Dad says.

Will and Amber are here. Amber has a book with rabbits in it.

"Look at this, Amber. This book has rabbits in it," says Peter.

27

Peter wants to go home to play.

"Can Amber come, please?" he says.

"Yes, Peter," says Dad.

"Can Will come home to play with cars, please?" Jane says.

"Yes," says Dad.

Mum is here with
the car.

Peter, Jane and Dad
get into the car.

They go home
to play.

"Come on in," say
Peter and Jane.

Amber and Peter play a rabbit game.

This rabbit hops.

That rabbit hops.

"Tess wants to play this rabbit game. Can you hop, Tess?" says Peter.

"Rabbits hop like this!" says Amber.

Will and Jane play with the cars.

This car goes.

That car goes.

Tess goes to play with the cars.

"Go and play with that ball, Tess," says Jane.

Will has rabbits
at home.

He has no dogs
at home.

"Please can we play with Tess?" says Will.

"Yes," Jane says.

47

"Yes!" says Will.

They get the ball and play with Tess, Amber and Peter.

49

"We like playing here and at home. We have rabbits at home," Will says.

"Can we go and play with the rabbits, please?" Peter says.

"Yes, please!" says Amber.

"We like rabbits!" says Jane.

Answer these questions about
the story.

1 What animal does Peter look at
   in the pet shop?

2 What book does Dad get for Mum?

3 Why does Will want to play
   with Tess?

4 Who has pet rabbits?